# MAXI THE LITTLE TAXI

BY Elizabeth Upton

PICTURES BY Henry Cole

SCHOLASTIC INC.

Mr. BUDDY'S TAXI SERVICE

LYRIC THEATER

THEATER

## MAXI THE TAXI

Was a dazzling sight—
Everything about him
Was flashy and bright!

He was little and yellow
And shiny and new.
On his first day of work
There was so much to do!

MAXI
THE
TAXI

His friend, Mr. Buddy,
Sent Max on his way.
"Drive safely," said Buddy.
"And have a great day!"

Max Z I P P E D here.

He Z I P P E D there.

He Z I P P E D everywhere—

From the park, to the river,
And back to the square.

He Z O O M E D up.

He Z O O M E D down.

He Z O O M E D all around town—

Splashing in every
big puddle he found!

Small sticky fingers
At stop after stop
Let ice cream and mustard
Go *plippity-plop.*

And outside the gates
Of an elegant park
A friendly pigeon
Left her mark!

Then up came a taxi gal—sparkling and neat
Who whispered to Max
    as they rolled down the street:
"You'd better wash up,
    Mr. Gooey-Goo,
Or *no one* will want to ride
    with you!"

When a fashionable lady
Waved for a ride,
Maxi Z O O M E D over—
But splashed her right side!

"My skirt!" screamed the lady.
"And look at you!
You're filthy and gooey—
And grimy, too!"

Soon all the people
Who needed a taxi
Took one quick look—
And walked right past Maxi.

Max was so sad,
Down streamed his tears,
And his *swish-swishing* wipers
Turned dirt into smears.

Then a boy with his mother,

Who waved, jumped, and hopped,

Were happy when

Maxi  Z O O M E D

over and

stopped.

"Yuck!" said the boy.
"I hope it's OK,
If we stop at that car wash
Across the way."

At the mouth of the car wash
Max screeched to a stop
Afraid he'd be eaten
Like a yellow gumdrop!

*Clink-clank!* Maxi's tires
Rolled onto the track,
But it was too late
For Max to turn back!

*Rumm-mum-mum*
Went the brushes.
*Pish-pish* went the spray,
Washing the grit and dirt away.

*Flip-flop* went the scrubbers—
*Blip-blop* went the suds—
And they tickled his muffler
And bumper and hubs.

"BEE-BEE-BEEP!"
laughed Max.

"BEE-BEE-BEEP!"

"BEE-BEE-BEEP!"

And out of the car wash he rolled
To the street!

Outside the streetlights
Shone down on Max . . .
And magically,
Max felt himself shining back!

He opened his windows—
Ready for flight—
And away they all went
Through the sparkling night!

"Welcome home!" said Mr. Buddy,
"You're right on time—
With no bumps or scratches—
Just look at you shine!"

"How was your day, Max?
Where have you been?
Here's an extra polish
While I tuck you in!"

Max told the whole story—
Of his kind, new friend,
And the big bath that splashed him—
Front, middle, and end!

And then, very tired,
Max sighed, *"Bee-de-beep . . ."*
And
     driftily,
          dreamily,
He fell fast asleep . . .